For Mom

First published in Belgium and Holland by Clavis Uitgeverij, Hasselt – Amsterdam, 2014
Copyright © 2014, Clavis Uitgeverij

English translation from the Dutch by Clavis Publishing Inc. New York
Copyright © 2015 for the English language edition: Clavis Publishing Inc. New York

Visit us on the web at www.clavisbooks.com

Chameleon Sees Colors written and illustrated by Anita Bijsterbosch
Original title: *Kameleon ziet kleuren*
Translated from the Dutch by Clavis Publishing

ISBN 978-1-60537-221-1

This book was printed in April 2015 at Wai Man Book Binding (China) Ltd. Flat A, 9/F., Phase 1,
Kwun Tong Industrial Centre, 472-484 Kwun Tong Road, Kwun Tong, Kowloon, H.K.

First Edition
10 9 8 7 6 5 4 3 2 1

Anita Bijsterbosch

Chameleon

sees colors

Clavis

NEW YORK

Chameleon thinks the whole world is black and white. And then one day he looks outside....

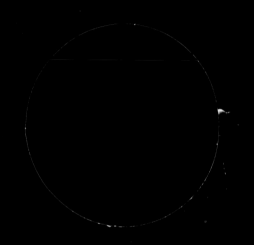

He sees…

... a red bird.

"Cheep, cheep," says the red bird.

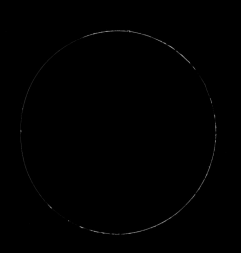

Then **Chameleon** sees...

... an orange tiger.

A moment later
Chameleon sees…

... a yellow
duckling.

"Quack, quack," says the yellow duckling.

A while later
Chameleon sees…

... a green cricket.

Then **Chameleon** sees…

... a blue owl.

"Whoo, whooohoo,"
says the blue owl.

Suddenly
Chameleon sees…

... a purple girl
chameleon!

"Hello,"
says the purple
girl chameleon.

How about you?

What's your favorite color?

"Hello," Chameleon answers quickly.

Chameleon is too shy to say so,
but he thinks purple is the prettiest
color he has ever seen!